Alice's Adventures in Wonderland is an Oxford story. In a boat on the river Cherwell, in the Deanery garden at Christ Church, the character of Alice took shape as Charles Dodgson, Fellow and Tutor in mathematics at Christ Church, Oxford, entertained Alice Liddell, the Dean's real-life daughter, with stories of his fictional character, Alice in Wonderland. Oxford landmarks pepper the story. The green Alice Door to the Deanery garden is the inspiration for the door through which Alice passes into a beautiful garden at the beginning of the story. The brass firedogs in the Hall, with their long necks, find an echo in the story in Alice's elongated neck. The extinct stuffed dodo at the Oxford University Museum of Natural History, which Dodgson visited with the Liddell children, is a direct link to the character of the Dodo.

Dodgson was expected to do serious work on mathematics, so when he published *Alice's Adventures in Wonderland*, he used a nom de plume, Lewis Carroll, to conceal his identity. The Bodleian Library, the main library of the University of Oxford, preferred to catalogue books under authors' real names, rather than pseudonyms. When the book came to the Bodleian Library in 1865, it was entered in the Library's catalogue under Dodgson, not Carroll. As the book became increasingly popular, speculation arose about the identity of the author. As the home of Alice, the record in the Bodleian catalogue carried authority, revealing to all the real name of the author, Charles Dodgson.

In this

DRINK ME

In this
Style
10/6